The Nutcracker
Activity Book

Written by Hazel Geatches

Illustrated by Kelly O'Neill

Song lyrics on page 16 by Wardour Studios

 Singing *    Reading   Speaking   Critical thinking

 Spelling   Writing   Listening *

*To complete these activities, listen to tracks 2, 3, and 4 of the Reader audio download available at www.ladybirdeducation.co.uk

Match the words to the pictures.

1 nutcracker

a

2 Candy Land

b

3 sleigh

c

4 present

d

5 dream

e

6 midnight

f

2 Look at the letters. Write the words.

1

s s m h C i t r a

Clara woke up under the
_____Christmas_____ tree.

2

o o c a h c l e t

They ate lots of candy, _____,
and cake.

3

h n i m t g d i

Clara woke up at _____.

4

m e r t y k o a

The _____ made a
present for Clara.

5

t e v f a r o i

The toymaker was Clara's
_____ friend.

3 Work with a friend. Talk about the two pictures. How are they different? 🗨

a

b

> In picture a, Clara is big.
> In picture b, Clara is small.

4 Look at the pictures.
Put a ✓ in the correct boxes.

1

a Christmas ✓
b Krismass ☐

2

a presen ☐
b present ☐

3

a sley ☐
b sleigh ☐

4

a midnight ☐
b midnite ☐

5

a dreem ☐
b dream ☐

6

a nutcracker ☐
b nutcraker ☐

5 Look and read.
Write the correct words on the lines.

| nice | small | favorite | beautiful |

1

"Oh, a nutcracker! What a ____nice____ present!" said Clara.

2

"Great," thought Clara. "My _____ friend is here!"

3

"Look at our _____ Christmas tree!" said Clara.

4

Clara said, "But why am I so _____?"

6 Listen, color, and draw.
Use the colors below. 🎧*

7 Look and read. Circle the correct words.

1  There was a **(party)** / **park** at Clara's house.

2  Clara's favorite **teacher** / **friend** was there.

3  Clara said **"Hello!"** / **"Goodbye!"** to the toymaker.

4  The toymaker made a **cake** / **present** for Clara.

5  The **nutcracker** / **chocolate** was a nice present.

6  The Sugarplum **Father** / **Fairy** was the Nutcracker's friend.

8 Match the two parts of the sentences.

1 "Let's sit and eat,"

chocolate, and cake.

2 They ate lots of candy,

an apple?" asked the Sugarplum Fairy.

3 "Would you like

said Clara.

4 "Yes, please!"

said the Sugarplum Fairy.

5 "Now," said the fairy,

"let's dance and sing."

9 **Work with a friend. Help the Nutcracker catch the mice. Use the words in the box.** 🗨

turn right   go straight   turn left   go to the end

Turn right. Then, turn left . . .

10 Look, match, and write the words.

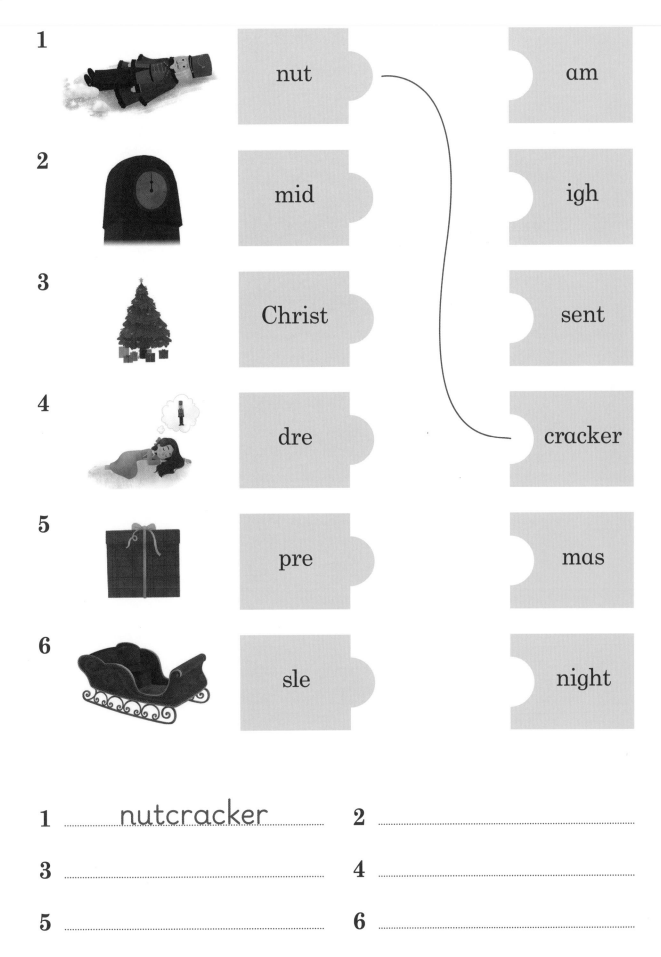

1   nut   am

2   mid   igh

3   Christ   sent

4   dre   cracker

5   pre   mas

6   sle   night

1   nutcracker   2 ....

3 ....   4 ....

5 ....   6 ....

Look and read. Write _T_ (true) or _F_ (false).

1 The Nutcracker's sleigh could fly. ....T.......

2 The sleigh flew below the houses. ....

3 Clara didn't like snow. ....

4 Clara and the Nutcracker played in the snow. ....

5 Then, they were hungry. ....

6 They didn't go to Candy Land. ....

12 Look and read. Circle the correct words.

1

a snow

b sleigh

c tree

2

a clock

b cake

c coat

3

a paper

b party

c present

4

a mouse

b house

c dress

13 Listen and write a—d. *

"It's beautiful. I love snow!" said Clara.

"Are you hungry now?" the Nutcracker asked.

"Oh, yes!" Clara smiled.

18

19

1 "It's beautiful." ....a........

2 "Oh, yes!" ....

3 "Are you hungry now?" ....

4 "I love snow!" ....

*To complete this activity, listen to track 3 of the Reader audio download available at **www.ladybirdeducation.co.uk**

14 **Draw a picture of the Nutcracker. Read the questions and write about the Nutcracker.**

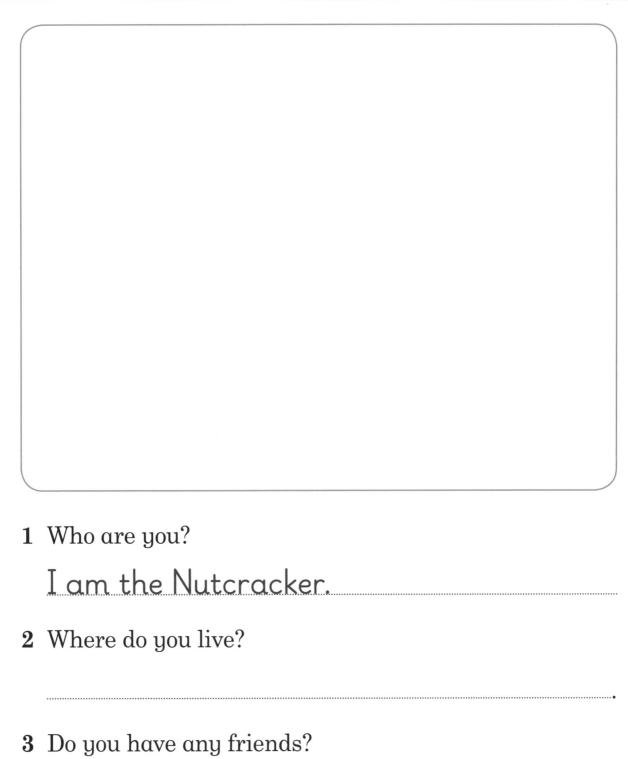

1 Who are you?

I am the Nutcracker.

2 Where do you live?

....

3 Do you have any friends?

....

4 Can you dance and sing?

....

15 Sing the song. *

The toymaker made a little present
For Clara on Christmas Day.
The party was at Clara's house,
And there was lots of fun and play.

She sat down under the Christmas tree,
And soon she closed her eyes.
The noise of the clock woke Clara up,
And what she saw was nice!

The Nutcracker, the Nutcracker!
He is Clara's little friend.
The Nutcracker, the Nutcracker!
He can stay to the end.

Clara was now very small.
She met an angry mouse.
The Nutcracker told her what to do.
Then they flew out of the house.

The Nutcracker, the Nutcracker!
He is Clara's little friend.
The Nutcracker, the Nutcracker!
He can stay to the end.

*To complete this activity, listen to track 4 of the Reader audio download available at www.ladybirdeducation.co.uk